How will Nancy unlock this case?

"Hi, Pudding Pie," Mr. Drew said. "Call for you. I think it's Bess."

Nancy sat up in bed and took the phone from her father. "Thanks, Daddy," she said. "Hi, Bess!" she said into the phone. "What's up?"

"I have really bad news!" Bess said in a teary-sounding voice. "It's the worst news ever!"

Nancy frowned. Bess sounded really upset.

"What's the matter, Bess?" Nancy asked her worriedly. "What's going on?"

"It's the key to the city," Bess burst out. "It's gone!"

The Nancy Drew Notebooks

# 1 The Slumber Party Secret	#27 Trouble Takes the Cake
# 2 The Lost Locket	#28 Thrill on the Hill
# 3 The Secret Santa	#29 Lights! Camera! Clues!
# 4 Bad Day for Ballet	#30 It's No Joke!
# 5 The Soccer Shoe Clue	#31 The Fine-Feathered Mystery
# 6 The Ice Cream Scoop	#32 The Black Velvet Mystery
# 7 Trouble at Camp Treehouse	#33 The Gumdrop Ghost
# 8 The Best Detective	#34 Trash or Treasure?
# 9 The Thanksgiving Surprise	#35 Third-Grade Reporter
#10 Not Nice on Ice	#36 The Make-Believe Mystery
#11 The Pen Pal Puzzle	#37 Dude Ranch Detective
#12 The Puppy Problem	#38 Candy Is Dandy
#13 The Wedding Gift Goof	#39 The Chinese New Year Mystery
#14 The Funny Face Fight	#40 Dinosaur Alert!
#15 The Crazy Key Clue	#41 Flower Power
#16 The Ski Slope Mystery	#42 Circus Act
#17 Whose Pet Is Best?	#43 The Walkie-talkie Mystery
#18 The Stolen Unicorn	#44 The Purple Fingerprint
#19 The Lemonade Raid	#45 The Dashing Dog Mystery
#20 Hannah's Secret	#46 The Snow Queen's Surprise
#21 Princess on Parade	#47 The Crook Who Took the Book
#22 The Clue in the Glue	#48 The Crazy Carnival Case
#23 Alien in the Classroom	#49 The Sand Castle Mystery
#24 The Hidden Treasures	#50 The Scarytales Sleepover
#25 Dare at the Fair	#51 The Old-Fashioned Mystery
#26 The Lucky Horseshoes	

Available from Simon & Schuster

THE
NANCY DREW
NOTEBOOKS®

#51

The Old-Fashioned Mystery

CAROLYN KEENE
ILLUSTRATED BY PAUL CASALE

Aladdin Paperbacks
New York   London   Toronto   Sydney   Singapore

First Aladdin Paperbacks edition December 2002

Copyright © 2002 by Simon & Schuster, Inc.

ALADDIN PAPERBACKS
An imprint of Simon & Schuster
Children's Publishing Division
1230 Avenue of the Americas
New York, NY 10020

The text of this book was set in Excelsior.

Printed in the United States of America
10 9 8 7 6 5 4 3 2 1

Library of Congress Control Number 2001098774

ISBN 0-7434-3766-7

LEO 3.99 BWI T

1
The Winner Is Announced

You three girls look very, very busy," Hannah Gruen remarked. She set a tray down on the dining room table with three mugs of hot chocolate on it.

Eight-year-old Nancy Drew glanced up from her composition notebook and smiled at Hannah. "We're working on an essay!"

"An *important* essay!" Nancy's best friend, Bess Marvin, chimed in.

"A *super*important essay!" Bess's cousin and Nancy's other best friend, George Fayne, added.

Nancy, Bess, and George were sitting around the Drews' dining room table. They were writing in their composition notebooks. Nearby, Nancy's Lab puppy, Chocolate Chip, lay asleep on the floor. Chip was wearing a special red holiday collar with velvet mistletoe on it.

Bess stopped writing. "How do you spell 'Heights'? Like in 'River Heights'?" she asked.

"H-E-I-G-H-T-S," Hannah replied.

"Oh," Bess and George said. Both girls began erasing like mad.

Even though Bess and George were cousins, they didn't really look alike. Bess had long, curly blond hair and blue eyes. George had dark brown hair and brown eyes. George's real name was Georgia, but hardly anyone ever called her that.

Hannah passed out the mugs of hot chocolate to the girls. Hannah had been the Drews' housekeeper since Nancy's mother died five years ago. But she was more than a housekeeper. Both Nancy and her father thought of her as a member of the family.

Nancy took a sip of her hot chocolate, which had a big mound of whipped cream on top. "Mmm, yummy! Thanks, Hannah!"

"You're very welcome," Hannah said. "So

what *is* this superimportant essay anyway?"

"We have to write an essay called, 'Why I Love River Heights,'" George explained. "It's a contest for elementary-school kids."

"The essays are due tomorrow," Nancy added.

"Well, no wonder you're all working so hard," Hannah said. "So what does the winner get?"

"Oh, it's the *best prize*!" Bess gushed. She licked whipped cream from her spoon. "You know the Holiday Streetwalk? Well, during it, whoever wins gets to give Mr. and Mrs. Santa Claus a key to the city!"

"Oh, my!" Hannah exclaimed.

Nancy smiled at the thought of the wonderful prize. A week from Sunday was the annual Holiday Streetwalk in downtown River Heights. Main Street would be filled with carolers, clowns, jugglers, and face painters. Storeowners would serve hot cider and cookies. Many grown-ups and kids would dress up in old-fashioned costumes.

But best of all, at nightfall, the mayor would turn on the lights of the big Christmas tree in front of City Hall. At the same time,

Santa Claus and Mrs. Claus would arrive on a horse-drawn sleigh.

And one lucky boy or girl would get to present Mr. and Mrs. Claus with a key to the city!

Will it be one of us? Nancy wondered, glancing at her two best friends.

Nancy knew there would be TV cameras and reporters there too. Whoever presented the key to Mr. and Mrs. Claus would be in the newspaper and on TV—just like a celebrity!

"Well, I guess that means you're all too busy to help me make Christmas cookies," Hannah said.

"We definitely won't be too busy to help you eat them!" Bess said eagerly.

Nancy and George giggled. Then the three girls turned back to their composition notebooks.

On the following Thursday, Nancy, Bess, and George walked into Mrs. Reynolds's classroom at Carl Sandburg Elementary School.

"I think today's going to be the day," Bess said in a low voice.

"The day for what?" George asked her.

"The day Mrs. Reynolds announces the winner of the essay contest, silly!" Bess reminded George.

Nancy glanced around the room, which was covered with holiday drawings and decorations. Their third-grade teacher, Mrs. Reynolds, was standing by her desk. She had a large white envelope in her hands.

"Bess! I think you're right," Nancy whispered excitedly. "Look at that envelope Mrs. Reynolds is holding!"

"I bet the winner's name is inside," George agreed.

"I hope it's one of us!" Bess squealed.

The three girls exchanged high fives, then sat down at their desks. Most of the other kids were already sitting down. Nancy waved at some of her friends: Julia Santos, Phoebe Archer, and Jenny March.

Nancy started to wave to Brenda Carlton, who sat several rows over. But Brenda just frowned at her, then turned away with a swish of her hair.

Brenda's father owned a big newspaper called *Today's Times*. Brenda had her own newspaper, which she created on her computer: the *Carlton News*. Brenda was usually snooty and mean to everyone, including Nancy. But Nancy refused to be snooty and mean back.

Nancy remembered just then that Mr. and Mrs. Carlton had invited Nancy and her father to a holiday party at their house on Saturday night. The Faynes and the Marvins had been invited too.

The first-period bell rang. Everyone stopped talking and faced front.

"Good morning, class," Mrs. Reynolds said with a smile. "Guess what I have in my hand?" She held up the white envelope.

"Free baseball cards for the whole class?" Jason Hutchings piped up. He and Mike Minnelli laughed.

Mrs. Reynolds shook her head. "Nope. These are the results of the 'Why I Love River Heights' essay contest."

Bess whirled around in her seat and grinned at Nancy.

"Remember, the contest was open to all elementary-school children in River Heights," Mrs. Reynolds reminded the class.

"So the winner might be someone we've never even heard of. Someone from River Heights Elementary School, for example."

"Or, it could be someone from this class!" Brenda said smugly. "Someone who's a really, really, *really* great writer!"

"Gee, like who?" Julia said, rolling her eyes.

Mrs. Reynolds opened the envelope and pulled out several sheets of paper. She scanned them quickly. Then her face lit up.

"Oh, my goodness! Brenda's right. The winner *is* someone from this class!" she said.

"I *knew* it!" Brenda exclaimed. She started to stand up.

"It's Bess Marvin!" Mrs. Reynolds announced.

Bess jumped out of her seat. "I won? Really? I won!" she shrieked.

Brenda frowned and sat back down.

"Yay, Bess!" Nancy cried out as the whole class started whistling and clapping.

"Way to go!" George cheered.

Mrs. Reynolds motioned for Bess to come to the front of the room. "Why don't you read your essay to the class, Bess?"

Beaming, Bess walked up front and took the sheet of paper from Mrs. Reynolds. She stared at the paper and cleared her throat.

"Go ahead, Bess," Mrs. Reynolds encouraged her.

Bess smiled nervously. She twirled and untwirled a strand of her long blond hair. Then she began to read.

"Ahem! 'Why I Love River Heights: I love River Heights because it's the best city in the whole world. It may not be as big as Chicago. But a city doesn't have to be big to be really great.

"'For example, River Heights has a cool park where my friends Nancy and George and I like to play. It has a skating rink. It has a candy factory called Zuckerman's Zonked Candy Factory.

"'It has an ice-cream shop, the Double Dip, that's awesome. It used to be *two* ice cream shops. But then—'"

But Bess wasn't able to finish her sentence. Just then, Brenda jumped up from her seat and pointed a finger at Bess.

"Bess Marvin cheated on her essay!" Brenda cried out. "And I can prove it!"

2

Danger on Ice

Nancy couldn't believe it. Brenda had just accused Bess of cheating on her "Why I Love River Heights" essay!

"That is a total lie!" Bess burst out. "I did *not* cheat on this essay! I wrote every word of it myself!"

"*You're* the liar!" Brenda yelled.

"*You're* the liar!" Bess yelled back.

Everyone in the class began whispering and buzzing. Mrs. Reynolds waved her arms and stepped between the two girls.

"All right, enough!" she said firmly. "Brenda, what on earth are you talking about? What do you mean, Bess cheated on her essay?"

"*Well*," Brenda said in a huff, putting her hands on her hips, "remember what she wrote about how River Heights isn't as big as Chicago? I wrote about that in my essay too. And remember that part about how the Double Dip used to be two ice cream shops? I said the *exact same thing*!"

"So we happened to write about some of the same stuff. That's not cheating!" Bess cried out.

Mrs. Reynolds frowned at Brenda. "Bess is right. If she had copied your essay word-for-word, that would have been cheating. But that's not what she did."

"But I'm telling you, she cheated!" Brenda protested.

"That's enough, Brenda!" Mrs. Reynolds said sharply. "I don't want to hear any more about cheating. In fact, I want you to apologize to Bess right now."

Brenda glared at Bess. "I'm sorry," she mumbled.

From where she sat, Nancy could see that

Brenda had her fingers crossed behind her back.

"Brenda was just mad because she wanted to win the contest herself," Bess declared.

"That Brenda is so mean," George agreed.

It was Friday, after school. The three girls were walking out of Muller's department store. They were carrying lots of shopping bags.

Mr. Marvin was right behind them. He had run into some people from his office and was talking to them about work.

The mayor's office had called Bess's parents last night. The mayor wanted Bess to be at the big Christmas tree at four o'clock, so they could have a dress rehearsal for Sunday's Holiday Streetwalk.

Nancy and George had come along so they could watch and cheer Bess on. Mr. Marvin had picked the three girls up at school. They'd spent the last hour Christmas shopping at different stores. Now it was time to head over to the tree.

The stores on Main Street were trimmed with pretty holiday decorations. The lampposts twinkled with tiny white lights. There were lots of people out and about, doing their holiday shopping.

The air was cold and crisp. The streets were covered with snow. Nancy rubbed her mittened hands together and said, "I hope we can take a hot-cider break soon!"

"Dad said he'll take us to the Cranberry Café as soon as we finish with the dress rehearsal," Bess said, her blue eyes sparkling.

Mr. Marvin said good-bye to the people from his office and joined the girls. "Sorry to keep you waiting. Come on, Bess, let's get over to your dress rehearsal!"

"Okay, Daddy!"

As they started down the sidewalk, Bess reached into one of her shopping bags. She pulled out a pair of fuzzy pink mittens. "I'm so happy Daddy bought me these at Muller's," she said to George and Nancy. "I'm going to wear them on Sunday."

They soon arrived at the Christmas tree. It was in an open area between Tiny Ted's Toy Shop and Star's Jewelers. Nancy thought the tree looked even taller than the one from last year. It was almost as tall as her house!

"All right, people, let's go, let's go, *let's go!*"

Nancy saw a tall, thin man standing in front of the Christmas tree. He was dressed in a long gray coat and a furry-looking hat. He was holding a clipboard in one hand and a cell phone in the other.

There were two young women running around. They had clipboards and cell phones too.

"Shelly, call Alice Stone over at *Today's Times,* and make sure she got the press release," the man barked at one of the women. "Annie, call WRIV and see which reporter they're sending over on Sunday. Make sure it's not that cranky one."

"Yes, Mr. Farnsworth," both women said at the same time. They started punching numbers into their cell phones.

The man named Mr. Farnsworth looked sharply at Nancy and her friends. "Who are you?"

Mr. Marvin stepped forward. "We got a call from the mayor's office asking us to be here. This is my daughter, Bess Marvin. She won the 'Why I Love River Heights' essay contest. This is her cousin George Fayne, and this is Nancy—"

"Oh, right, yes, yes, yes." Mr. Farnsworth glanced down impatiently at his clipboard. He checked something off with a pen. "I'm Franklin Farnsworth, the deputy mayor. Let's get started, shall we? Which one of you is Bess again?"

"I'm Bess!" Bess waved her hand. "Where's the mayor? And where are Mr. and Mrs. Claus?"

"I'm standing in for the mayor. He'll be here Sunday. And the Clauses won't be here till Sunday either. Let's see, we can use . . ." Mr. Farnsworth peered around. "Shelly, you be Santa Claus! And Annie, you be Mrs. Claus! My assistants," he explained to Nancy and the others.

The two young women rushed over to Mr. Farnsworth.

Bess leaned over to Nancy. "Those women don't *look* like Mr. and Mrs. Santa Claus," she whispered doubtfully.

"I know, I know. But just pretend," Nancy whispered back.

Nancy, George, and Mr. Marvin moved off

to the side as the dress rehearsal began. Mr. Farnsworth had Bess stand right next to the Christmas tree.

"On Sunday evening a big crowd will gather around the tree," Mr. Farnsworth explained to Bess. "The mayor will give a speech. At the end of the speech, he'll flick a switch, and the lights on the Christmas tree will come on. Then he'll hand you the key to the city."

Mr. Farnsworth reached into his pocket and pulled out a black velvet bag. He handed the bag to Bess. "You will then open the bag and pull out the key. . . . Go ahead, do it."

Bess opened the bag and pulled out a big gold key. She beamed. "Wow, it's beautiful! It looks old."

"It *is* old," Mr. Farnsworth said. "It's an antique."

"That means it's *super*old," Nancy whispered to George. George nodded.

"Just as you're pulling out the key, Bess, Mr. and Mrs. Claus will drive up in their sleigh," Mr. Farnsworth went on. He turned. "Shelly! Annie! Pretend you're driving up in a sleigh!"

Shelly and Annie glanced at each other. Then they held up their hands as if they were holding reins. They started skipping over to where Bess was standing.

"Great! Fabulous!" Mr. Farnsworth said, looking pleased. "Now, Bess, you should—"

Mr. Farnsworth stopped. His cell phone was ringing, and he answered it with a frown. "What now? Hello, Farnsworth here. What do you mean, the files are gone?"

Mr. Farnsworth sighed, then hung up. "I have a . . . little emergency to take care of. I must leave right away. Can the rest of you stay and run through this a couple more times? Do the exact same thing, except in the end, you, Bess, need to hand the key to Santa Shelly. Mr. Marvin, maybe you could play the part of the mayor."

"No problem," Mr. Marvin said. "Mayor Marvin. I like that." He smiled and straightened his hat.

"You can hang on to the key until Sunday," Mr. Farnsworth told Bess and Mr. Marvin. "Just be very careful with it—it's one-of-a-kind. Keep it in a safe place."

"Okey-dokey!" Bess said, nodding.

Nancy turned to George. "Bess is doing great!" she whispered.

"There are going to be zillions of people here on Sunday," George whispered back. "I hope she doesn't get nervous."

"It's good she gets to practice now," Nancy whispered.

After Mr. Farnsworth left, Bess, Mr. Marvin, Shelly, and Annie started to run through everything one more time. People stopped on the sidewalk to watch.

Shelly and Annie pretended to ride up to the Christmas tree on their "sleigh." Bess smiled and reached into the black velvet bag to hand the key to Shelly.

"I hereby present you with the key to the city," Bess began.

But just then, a snowball flew through the air and hit her square in the back. Bess cried out and stumbled forward. Then she lost her balance on a patch of ice—and fell to the ground!

3

Missing!

Bess sat up on the patch of ice. She looked really mad.

"Who did that? Who threw a snowball at me?" she demanded as she shoved the key back in its bag.

Mr. Marvin rushed up to her. "Are you okay, pumpkin?" he asked worriedly.

"I'm fine, Daddy," Bess replied, reaching around to rub her back. "I want to know who did that though!"

Nancy glanced over at Tiny Ted's Toy Shop. The snowball had come from that direction.

She saw two boys standing in front of Tiny Ted's. She recognized one of them. His

20

name was Gary. He went to River Heights Elementary School.

Gary and his friend were pointing at Bess and snickering. Nancy put her hands on her hips and marched up to them.

"Did *you* throw that snowball at Bess?" Nancy asked them angrily.

Gary grinned. "Who, us?"

"Why would we do a thing like that?" the other boy said, giggling.

"We wouldn't want Miss Contest Winner to get all covered with snow!" Gary said.

Nancy glanced down at Gary's mittens. They had snow all over them—as though he had just been making snowballs.

"You *did* do it, didn't you?" Nancy said accusingly.

Just then Mr. Marvin marched up to Gary and the other boy. Bess and George were right behind him.

"What's your name, young man?" Mr. Marvin asked Gary. "I'd like to have a talk with your parents."

Gary and the other boy glanced at each other. Then they took off running down the sidewalk.

"Hey!" Mr. Marvin called out. He sighed and turned to Nancy. "Do *you* know that boy's name?"

"It's Gary something," Nancy replied. "He goes to River Heights Elementary School. I don't know the other boy's name."

"Well, the next time I see him, I'm going to throw a snowball back at him," Bess said with a pout.

"You'll do no such thing, pumpkin," Mr. Marvin told her.

"That Gary boy's probably mad because someone from *his* school didn't win the contest," George guessed. "Sour grapes!"

"Sort of like Brenda," Nancy agreed.

When the dress rehearsal was over, Mr. Marvin took the girls to the Cranberry Café for some hot cider.

Then they went to the Ye Olde Antique Shoppe.

As they walked inside, Nancy leaned over to Bess and whispered, "Do you have the key to the city in a safe place?"

Bess hugged her Muller's shopping bag to her chest. "Uh-huh, it's right in here."

Nancy nodded. "Good!"

Mr. Ortiz, the owner of the Ye Olde Antique Shoppe, came out from behind the counter. He was tall and slender with grayish-black hair and tortoiseshell glasses.

"Welcome!" he called out in a booming voice. "Can I help you lovely ladies find something? Oh, and you too, sir," he said, winking at Mr. Marvin.

"My dad wants to find a pretty antique necklace for my mom," Bess piped up.

"Oh, well, I think we may have a few of those," Mr. Ortiz said.

"We just came from a dress rehearsal," George said proudly.

"A dress rehearsal? You mean for a play?" Mr. Ortiz asked the girls.

Nancy shook her head. "Uh-uh. It was a dress rehearsal for Sunday night at the River Heights Holiday Streetwalk. Bess won an essay contest, so she gets to present Mr. and Mrs. Santa Claus with the key to the city!" She pointed to Bess.

"I even get to keep the key until Sunday night," Bess said, holding up her shopping bag.

Mr. Ortiz looked impressed. "Well, my goodness!"

The door opened just then. A family bustled in. Nancy recognized Melissa Adams from school, and her mother and father, too. The three of them were carrying lots of shopping bags.

Mrs. Adams was also holding a small girl in her arms. The girl was squirming and fidgeting.

"Quiet, Mandy," Mrs. Adams shushed. "Let Mommy and Daddy shop for a few minutes."

"Hey, Melissa," Nancy called out.

Melissa's eyes lit up. "Oh, hey, Nancy! Hey, Bess and George!"

"Hi, Melissa," said Bess and George.

"Down!" Mandy said, thrashing around in her mother's arms. "Mandy get down!"

"Okay, okay," Mrs. Adams sighed, setting Mandy down. "Don't touch anything though. No touching!"

"No touching!" Mandy squeaked. She toddled across the room. She stopped and picked up an antique pillow, then dropped it on the floor. She started to pick up a vase.

"I've got her," Mr. Adams said quickly to

his wife. He set his shopping bags down and ran after Mandy.

"Are you guys shopping for antiques?" Nancy asked Melissa.

"My mom is looking for a silver picture frame," Melissa explained.

Nancy told Melissa all about Bess's dress rehearsal. "Wow, that is so cool!" Melissa said when Nancy had finished her story.

"Hey, guys, check this out! A real antique feather boa!" Bess exclaimed. She set her shopping bags down and picked up a black boa that was draped over a velvet chair. She put it around her neck. "How do I look?"

"Like a movie star," Melissa said, giggling. "You should wear that on Sunday night!"

A few minutes later Mr. Marvin gathered up the girls. He held up a small Ye Olde Antique Shoppe bag. "I found the perfect thing for your mom, Bess. Why don't we make a quick stop to the Book Nook?"

"Sure, Daddy," Bess said.

The four of them said good-bye to Mr. Ortiz and to Melissa and her parents, too. Then they headed down the street to the Book Nook.

The Book Nook was a cozy little bookstore filled with new and old books. Nancy went there often with her dad.

The owner, Julia Sandback, waved from behind the counter. She was tall and skinny and had fiery red hair.

"Hi, Ms. Sandback!" The girls waved.

Nancy noticed that Brenda Carlton was there with her father. They were looking at cookbooks.

Mr. Carlton and Mr. Marvin exchanged greetings. "We're looking forward to your party this Saturday!" Mr. Marvin said with a smile.

Brenda pretended not to see Nancy and her friends.

"Doing some holiday shopping?" Ms. Sandback asked Nancy and her friends.

"Yup!" George replied.

"Plus, we just came from a dress rehearsal!" Bess added.

Bess told Ms. Sandback all about the ceremony. Out of the corner of her eye Nancy saw that Brenda was eavesdropping. Brenda didn't look pleased.

Just then, Nancy saw something else. Gary

from River Heights Elementary School was standing behind a display of gardening books. He seemed to be eavesdropping on Bess's conversation too!

"Hey you!" Nancy called out. "Gary! You're the one who threw the snowball at Bess!"

Mr. Marvin stopped talking to Mr. Carlton and turned around. He marched up to Gary. "You! I want to have a word with you!"

A tall man with red hair emerged from the history section and put his hand on Gary's shoulder. "I'm Gary's father. What's going on?" he demanded.

Mr. Marvin told Gary's father about the snowball incident. Bess looked mad, like she wanted to say something to Gary. Nancy took Bess's arm and pulled her over to the children's section. George followed.

"Let's go pick out books to ask Santa Claus for," Nancy suggested.

Bess broke into a smile. "Great idea! We can even tell Santa Claus in person on Sunday night!"

Bess picked up a book of fairy tales. She and George started looking through it.

Nancy peeked over her shoulder. Mr.

Marvin was still talking to Gary's father.

I hope this is the last time Gary does something mean to Bess, Nancy thought.

Later that night Nancy yawned and crawled under the covers. She was exhausted from all that shopping.

There was a knock at her door. "Yes? Who is it?" Nancy called out.

Carson Drew, Nancy's father, poked his head through the door. He held up a cordless phone.

"Hi, Pudding Pie," he said. "Pudding Pie" was Mr. Drew's special nickname for his daughter. "Call for you. I think it's Bess."

Nancy sat up in bed and took the phone from her father. "Thanks, Daddy," she said. "Hi, Bess!" she said into the phone.

"I have really bad news!" Bess said in a teary-sounding voice. "It's the worst news ever!"

Nancy frowned. Bess sounded really upset.

"What's the matter, Bess?" Nancy asked her worriedly. "What's going on?"

"It's the key to the city," Bess burst out. "It's gone!"

4

The Search for the Key

Nancy gasped. How could the key to the city be gone?

"Okay, slow down," Nancy said into the phone. "What do you mean, the key to the city is gone?"

"It's just gone!" Bess cried out.

"Start from the beginning," Nancy suggested.

Bess took a deep breath. "O-Okay," she began. "After Daddy and I dropped you guys off, we came home. I put all my shopping bags on my bed. Then we had dinner. After dinner we watched some TV. And then before I got ready to go to bed, I went through my shopping bags. I wanted to look at the stuff we bought."

"Then what happened?" Nancy prompted.

"The bag from Muller's was missing!" Bess explained. "You know the one with my pink mittens? The one that had the key in it? It wasn't with the other bags!"

"Was the bag there when you brought all your *other* bags into the house?" Nancy asked Bess.

"I don't know. I don't remember. I was carrying a whole bunch of bags," Bess said. "Anyway, I told Daddy what happened, and we looked in the car right away. But the Muller's bag wasn't there. We looked all over the house and even the yard. No bag!"

"Hmmm," Nancy said.

"This is awful!" Bess said tearfully. "I've lost the key to the city. Mr. Farnsworth is going to be so mad at me. So will the mayor. So will Mr. and Mrs. Santa Claus!"

"Don't worry, Bess. We'll find it," Nancy reassured her friend. But deep down, she wasn't sure. What could have happened to the key?

* * * *

31

"Okay, let's go over everything that happened," Nancy said.

It was Saturday morning. Nancy, Bess, and George were sitting on Bess's bed. They were having an emergency meeting about the missing key.

"You had the bag after we left Muller's," George pointed out. "You showed us your pink mittens, remember?"

Bess nodded. "I remember."

"Then we went to the Ye Olde Antique Shoppe," Nancy reminded her friends. "Could you have left the bag there?"

"Maybe," Bess said. She picked up a teddy bear and hugged it to her chest. "My mom and dad tried to call Mr. Ortiz this morning—and Ms. Sandback, too. But their stores don't open till ten o'clock on Saturdays."

"Don't forget the Cranberry Café," George said. "We went there right after we left the dress rehearsal."

Bess shook her head. "But I had the bag after we left there. I remember, because I looked inside to make sure the key was there."

"Oh," Nancy said.

Nancy twirled a lock of her hair and looked out the window. It had started to snow. The trees and grass were covered with white. It looked very Christmassy.

Nancy loved solving mysteries. She had solved lots of mysteries before. And here was a really important mystery—the mystery of the missing key! She knew she could do it—if she just put her mind to it.

Nancy looked at her friends. "We're going to find the key by tomorrow night," she told Bess. "I have a plan."

"You do?" Bess asked eagerly.

Just then Mrs. Marvin popped her head through the door. She had a worried look on her face. "Bess, I think we should call the mayor right now and let him know about the missing key."

Bess jumped up from the bed and wrapped her arms around her mother. "Nancy thinks she can find the key," she said breathlessly. "Please, can we wait to call the mayor? Nancy's an awesome detective. I know she can find it!"

Mrs. Marvin frowned. "I don't know . . . ," she said, hesitating.

"Please, Mommy?" Bess begged.

"Oh, all right," Mrs. Marvin said finally. "But if the key doesn't turn up by tomorrow evening before the tree-lighting ceremony, we *have* to let the mayor know. Understood?"

"Yes, Mommy!" Bess promised.

"So what's your plan?" George asked Nancy.

Nancy stood up. "I think we should go visit Ms. Sandback and Mr. Ortiz. We can ask them if they've seen the bag. And we can look around their stores, too."

"That's a good idea," Mrs. Marvin said. She dug into her jeans pocket and pulled out a set of car keys. "I'll drive!"

Nancy, Bess, George, and Mrs. Marvin stopped by the Book Nook first. Julia Sandback was just opening up.

"Good morning!" Ms. Sandback said merrily. "You're my first customers for the day."

"We're not shopping today," Bess told her.

"We're looking for something we lost," George added.

Ms. Sandback raised her eyebrows. "Oh? What did you girls lose?"

"A shopping bag from Muller's department store," Nancy explained. "A small one. Did you see it?"

"We might have left it here last night," Bess said.

Ms. Sandback frowned and glanced around. "Hmm, a small Muller's bag. I don't think you left it here, girls."

"Could we look around the store?" Nancy asked her.

Ms. Sandback smiled. "Of course!"

Nancy, Bess, and George began searching up and down the aisles.

They finally got to the last aisle in the store. But they still hadn't found the bag.

Bess bit her lip. "It's not here," she said in a trembling voice.

Nancy put her arm around her friend's shoulders. "Don't worry, Bess. It could still be at Mr. Ortiz's store."

They said good-bye to Ms. Sandback. She promised to keep her eyes open for the bag. Then they left and started down the street toward the Ye Olde Antique Shoppe.

Along the way they passed the big Christmas tree. There were four kids from the junior high school decorating it. Nancy recognized Howard Nakamoto, who lived up the street.

Howard and another boy were up on a ladder. They were wrapping a string of lights around the tree. Two girls were hanging silver and gold decorations on the branches.

"Let's walk faster!" Bess whispered to Nancy. "Seeing the Christmas tree reminds me of . . . you know!"

The girls and Mrs. Marvin soon reached the Ye Olde Antique Shoppe. Mr. Ortiz was inside. He was standing behind the counter, polishing a brass owl with a cloth.

"Hello again!" he called out to the girls. "You brought me a new customer, I see." He smiled at Mrs. Marvin.

"We need to ask you something, Mr. Ortiz," Nancy said. "We might have left something here yesterday. Have you seen a Muller's shopping bag?"

"One of the small ones," George piped up.

Mr. Ortiz pushed his glasses up his nose. "A small Muller's shopping bag . . . hmm."

"With a pair of mittens in it," Bess added.

"Oh, yes!" Mr. Ortiz nodded. "I did find

something like that last night. It was over there on the floor, next to the marble statue."

"You found it?" Bess broke into a smile. "Yay, Mr. Ortiz! You're our hero!" She began jumping up and down.

Nancy and George grabbed Bess's hands. "This is great!" George exclaimed. "Mystery solved!"

"That was the fastest mystery we've ever solved," Nancy said, laughing.

Mr. Ortiz disappeared through a doorway. He came back out a minute later and handed Bess a small Muller's shopping bag.

Bess reached into it eagerly. Then she pulled out . . . a pair of *red* mittens.

Her face fell. "These aren't my mittens! My mittens are pink!"

Nancy peeked into the bag. "And the key isn't in there either."

"Huh," Mr. Ortiz said, rubbing his chin. "That must be someone else's bag, then."

"So you didn't find another Muller's bag in the store?" Bess asked him.

Mr. Ortiz shook his head. "Nope, no other bag."

"Let's look around," Nancy said to George

and Bess. "I bet your bag is in here somewhere, Bess!"

"Just be careful back in the corner. I just got in some antique china and crystal, and it's very fragile," Mr. Ortiz warned.

"Okay, Mr. Ortiz," Nancy promised.

Nancy led her friends through the cluttered aisles of the store. They looked under feather boas. They looked behind dusty old paintings. They looked inside big brass trunks.

But Bess's bag was nowhere to be found.

"I guess it's not here," Bess said, looking disappointed.

"I guess we'd better give up and look somewhere else," George suggested.

"I guess you guys are right," Nancy said. She turned and started walking toward the front of the store where Mr. Ortiz and Mrs. Marvin were talking about antique watches.

And then Nancy noticed something . . . and stopped in her tracks.

Against one of the walls was a glass case. And inside the glass case were rows and rows of antique keys, lined up in neat rows.

Could one of them be the key to the city? Nancy wondered.

5

The Holiday Party

ancy called Bess and George over to the case full of antique keys.

"Look!" Nancy said in a low voice.

Bess and George stood on either side of Nancy. They peered into the case.

"Oh, my gosh!" Bess exclaimed.

"Is the key to the city in there?" George asked Nancy.

Nancy bent down. "Bess, you would know better than George and me. What did the key look like, exactly? Do you see it in there?"

Bess bent down next to her. "It was big and gold. The top of it was kind of oval-shaped. And it had the letters R. H. on it, for 'River Heights.' The letters were pretty and old-fashioned looking."

Nancy studied all the keys in the case. She didn't see a key that fit Bess's description.

"I don't see it in there," Nancy said after a minute. "Do you?" she asked Bess and George.

Bess and George shook their heads.

"Did you girls find something?"

Nancy whirled around. Mr. Ortiz was standing behind the three of them.

"Uh, we were just—," Bess stammered.

"Looking around," George finished.

"I thought you girls were searching for a shopping bag," Mr. Ortiz said in a stern voice. "There are no shopping bags in that case."

"We wanted to make sure to look everywhere," Nancy said quickly. "Thank you, Mr. Ortiz! Let us know if you ever find that bag!"

Then she grabbed Bess and George's arms and steered them toward the front door. Nancy didn't like how serious he sounded, and she wanted to get out of there before Mr. Ortiz asked them any more questions.

* * * *

"You don't think Mr. Ortiz stole the key to the city, do you?" Bess asked Nancy. "He's so nice!"

Nancy, Bess, and George were at the Double Dip. They were sitting at a booth in the corner, drinking hot chocolate. Mrs. Marvin had dropped them off there while she ran some errands.

Nancy took a sip of her hot chocolate. "I don't know. He might have. He sells antique keys in his store. Maybe he stole the key so he could sell it!"

"But it wasn't in the case," George pointed out.

"Maybe he already sold it," Nancy replied.

"Or maybe he secretly took it out of the case when he saw us coming," Bess added.

George looked doubtful. "I don't know. He's so nice. He doesn't seem like a thief."

"I know what you mean," Nancy said. "Still, we should put him on the suspect list since he does sell keys."

"And he seemed like he was trying to get us away from the case," Bess pointed out.

Nancy nodded. "We'd better write all this stuff down. It's getting complicated."

She reached into her backpack and pulled out a blue notebook. It was a special detective notebook her father had given her for writing down clues.

She turned to a fresh page, uncapped her purple pen, and began writing:

THE CASE OF THE MISSING KEY SUSPECTS:

<u>1. Mr. Ortiz at the Ye Olde Antique Shoppe</u>
*Bess had the key with her when we were in his store last night.
*He sells antique keys in his store.
*He didn't want us near the case where he keeps the keys.

Nancy glanced up from the notebook. "Any other suspects?"

"That mean Brenda Carlton!" Bess said, waving her spoon in the air. "She wanted to win the essay contest for herself. Maybe she stole the key because she was mad about not winning!"

George nodded. "She was in the Book Nook last night, remember? She could have stolen the shopping bag then."

"That sneak!" Bess said with a pout.

"Come on, Bess. We don't know Brenda's our thief. Not yet, anyway." Then Nancy thought of something. "What about that boy, Gary? The one who threw the snowball at you? He was at the Book Nook too!"

"Yeah, maybe *he* took the key!" Bess said, nodding. "Write that down, Nancy!"

Nancy picked up her purple pen and wrote under "Suspects":

2. <u>Brenda Carlton</u>
*She was at the Book Nook last night at the same time as us.
*She was mad about not winning the contest.
3. <u>Gary from River Heights Elementary School</u>
*He was at the Book Nook last night too.
*He and his friend were making fun of Bess about the contest.
*Maybe he was mad that someone from his school didn't win the contest.

Nancy put her pen down. "I just thought of something," she said slowly. "We're going to see at least one of our suspects tonight."

"Who?" Bess demanded.

"Brenda!" Nancy replied with a grin. "We're all invited to the Carltons' holiday party, remember?"

"Oh, yeah," George said, her brown eyes twinkling.

"If Brenda's our thief, maybe we'll have the key back tonight!" Nancy exclaimed.

That night, Nancy walked into the Carltons' house with her arm linked through her father's. She was dressed in a red velvet party dress, white tights, and black patent-leather shoes. Her father was dressed in a dark gray suit.

"Wow, this is some party, Pudding Pie," Mr. Drew said, whistling.

"Definitely!" Nancy agreed.

The inside of the Carltons' house had been transformed into a holiday wonderland. There were white icicle lights hanging from the ceilings. The wood floors were covered with fake glittery snow. There were wreaths and mistletoe and garlands everywhere.

An enormous Christmas tree stood in the center of the living room. It was covered with real candles and strings of popcorn and cranberries. Next to the tree was a big wooden sleigh full of presents.

The place was jam-packed with people. Nancy guessed that there might be a hundred guests there.

"Welcome, Carson, thanks for coming!" A tall, dark-haired man strolled across the room and shook Mr. Drew's hand.

"You remember Mr. Carlton, Nancy," Mr. Drew said.

Nancy shook Mr. Carlton's hand. "Hi, Mr. Carlton. Thank you for inviting us to your party."

"Mrs. Carlton is in the kitchen getting more hors d'oeuvres," Mr. Carlton said. "And Brenda's over there by the punch bowl. I'm sure she'd love to see you, Nancy!"

Nancy wasn't so sure about that. But she nodded and said, "Okay, Mr. Carlton. Thanks!"

Nancy started across the room. At the buffet table, she ran into Bess and George.

They were helping themselves to some cupcakes and apple cider.

Bess was wearing a powder-blue dress and a white bow in her hair. George was wearing a navy-blue dress with gold buttons.

"Hi, guys!" Nancy said, waving. "When did you get here?"

"About ten minutes ago," Bess replied. "*My* mom and dad and I came with George and *her* mom and dad."

A maid came by with a tray. "Would you care for a canapé?" she asked the girls.

George stared at the tray. "What's a can-a-pay?"

"Well, canapés can be different things," the maid replied. "These are crackers covered with salmon eggs and cream cheese."

Bess wrinkled her nose. "Salmon eggs? No, thank you!"

After the maid walked away, Nancy turned to Bess and George. "I was thinking," she said in a low voice. "Instead of giving Brenda the third degree about the missing key, maybe we should try a different plan."

"Like what?" George asked her.

"Like, why don't you two go talk to her

47

and keep her busy?" Nancy suggested. "While you do that, I'll go peek in her room."

"Nancy, that's brilliant!" Bess exclaimed. Then she made a face. "There's just one problem."

"What?" Nancy asked her.

"We have to talk to Brenda!" Bess grimaced.

Nancy giggled. "You can do it. I know you can! Just don't let her come upstairs before I'm back, okay?"

"But what if she goes upstairs anyway?" Bess asked.

"Then I'll hide in the closet," Nancy joked.

"Okay," George said.

Nancy waved good-bye to her friends and headed out into the hallway. Then she went up the stairs to the second floor.

There were lots and lots of doors. They were all closed. She wondered which one was Brenda's bedroom.

She came across one that had the initials B. C. on it. The letters were red with white polka dots.

That must be Brenda's room! Nancy thought.

She put her ear to the door and listened. She didn't hear anything. She opened the door and went inside.

Brenda's room had a big four-poster bed with a lacy white canopy over it. There was a wooden desk with a purple computer on top of it.

Walking on tiptoe, Nancy looked around the room. She peeked in the closet. She peeked under the bed. There was no sign of the Muller's shopping bag—or the key.

She was just about to give up when she saw something poking out from behind the purple computer.

Nancy glanced behind the computer. It was a small Muller's shopping bag!

But before she could pick it up, she heard footsteps outside the door. She clamped her hand over her mouth and tried not to panic.

Was she about to get caught snooping in Brenda's room?

6

Bad News

The footsteps came closer. It sounded like more than one person.

Nancy looked around frantically for a place to hide. She was about to get caught snooping in Brenda's room!

The closet! she thought.

Nancy made a beeline for the closet and shut the door behind her. She wedged herself in the back, behind a bunch of dresses. Just then, she heard the door to the bedroom open—and more footsteps.

"Bess! George! Why are you two following me?"

Nancy recognized Brenda's voice.

"We just *had* to see your room!" That was George's voice.

"It's *sooooooo* beautiful!" That was Bess.

"Wow, check out that purple computer! That's the coolest computer I've ever seen!" said George.

"Well, uh, thanks." Brenda sounded surprised that Bess and George were being so friendly to her. "I just need to get my velvet hat out of my closet. It matches my dress."

Closet? Nancy clapped her hand over her mouth to keep from making any noise. This was not good! She was about to get caught!

The doorknob to the closet turned. Nancy gulped.

"Oh, but that dress looks great without a hat," Bess said quickly.

The doorknob stopped turning.

"You think so?" Brenda said.

"Bess is right!" George piped up. "You should definitely go hatless. Besides, you have really pretty hair. You don't want to cover it up with a hat."

"Really?" Brenda said.

"Let's go back downstairs! Brenda, why

don't you show us that Ping-Pong table you were talking about?" Bess suggested.

"Hmm, okay, maybe."

Their footsteps went away. Nancy poked her head out the door. The three girls were gone.

"Whew!" she said to herself.

Nancy went back to Brenda's computer and took a quick look at the Muller's shopping bag. She sighed in disappointment. The only thing inside was a red silk scarf. There were no pink mittens, and there was no key, either.

Nancy put the bag back and headed downstairs. She found Brenda, Bess, and George in the family room.

Nancy glanced at Bess. Bess mouthed the words: "Did you find the key?" Nancy shook her head.

Brenda grinned at Nancy. "Where have *you* been? I bet I could beat you at table tennis with one hand tied behind my back!" she bragged.

"No, thanks," Nancy said to Brenda. "Hey, remember when we saw you at the Book Nook yesterday?"

Brenda narrowed her eyes. "Yeah? What about it?"

"You didn't happen to see a little shopping bag there, did you? From Muller's department store?" Nancy asked her.

Brenda frowned. "What are you talking about?"

Nancy was about to say something else when Mr. Marvin walked into the room. He was holding a glass of punch.

"Oh, there you are, pumpkin," he said cheerfully to Bess. "You girls having fun?"

"Yes, Daddy," Bess said, nodding.

"Say, have you girls had any luck tracking down the key to the city?" Mr. Marvin asked Nancy.

Brenda's eyes grew enormous. "The key to the city is *missing*?" she demanded.

"*Daddy!*" Bess whispered, putting her finger to her lips.

Brenda glanced at Bess and then at Mr. Marvin. She broke into a gleeful smile.

Oh, no! Nancy thought. *Now Brenda knows. And she can't keep a secret!*

On the other hand, Nancy realized something important: Brenda didn't know that the key was missing. Which meant that she didn't steal it!

By Sunday at four o'clock, downtown River Heights was jam-packed with people. The Holiday Streetwalk had officially begun.

Almost everyone was dressed in old-fashioned costumes. There were women in velvet dresses and capes. There were men in stroller coats and top hats.

Nancy and her friends were dressed in old-fashioned clothes too. Nancy wore a brown velvet coat and matching hat, with a red bow at her neck. Bess wore a fancy beige coat with a black muffler. George wore a striped dress with a red velvet smock over it.

Even Chip was dressed in a costume. She was wearing a red-and-white sweater.

"This would be so much fun," Bess whispered to her friends, "if it weren't for the fact that the key is still missing!"

The three girls had spent the day trying to find the key. They had gone back to the Book Nook and the Ye Olde Antique Shoppe with Mr. Marvin. They had walked up and down Main Street, just in case Bess might have dropped the bag somewhere. They had even gone to the lost-and-found department at the River Heights Welcome Center.

But there was no sign of the key anywhere.

Bess glanced over her shoulder. Her parents, the Faynes, Carson Drew, and Hannah were walking a few feet behind the girls.

"My parents said that we *have* to find the key by the time the tree-lighting ceremony starts," Bess whispered. "Otherwise, we have to tell the mayor and Mr. Farnsworth. Dad thinks they'll probably cancel my part in the ceremony and just have the mayor greet Santa and Mrs. Claus! Everyone will be super-mad at me when they find out that I lost the key!" She sniffled.

"Don't worry, Bess, we'll think of something," Nancy whispered. "We still have a little time."

"Yeah, but not much," George pointed out. "It's already starting to get dark."

Nancy glanced around. Downtown looked so pretty with twinkling lights and holiday decorations everywhere. Storeowners were standing out on the sidewalk, passing out cookies and cups of hot cider. There was a group of carolers on the corner, singing Christmas carols.

Just then, Gary—the boy from River Heights Elementary School—walked by. His parents were dressed in costumes. Gary was dressed in jeans and a ski parka.

Nancy stopped. "Hey, Gary!"

Gary stopped. He glanced at Bess and blushed. "Hey," he mumbled.

His father put his hand on his shoulder. "Gary, isn't there something you want to say to Miss Marvin?"

Gary's face turned even redder. "I'm sorry about hitting you with that snowball," he said to Bess. "It . . . was a dumb thing to do."

"I think Gary was upset because he wanted someone from his school to win the contest," Gary's mother told Mr. and Mrs. Marvin. "You know, like *him*."

"Yeah, whatever," Gary said, looking embarrassed. "Anyway, I'm sorry. I won't do that again."

"Apology accepted," Bess told him.

Nancy turned to Gary. "Hey, wait a minute.

You were at the Book Nook on Friday night. Did you see a small Muller's shopping bag there? And did you maybe pick it up by accident?"

Gary frowned and shrugged. "No."

"Not even a key?" George piped up.

Gary frowned again. "Huh?"

"I don't think he knows anything about the key," Bess whispered to Nancy.

"Yeah, I think you're right," Nancy whispered back.

Nancy and her friends bid Gary and his parents good-bye. They started heading down the sidewalk again when a voice rang out behind them.

"Bess? Bess Marvin?"

Nancy, Bess, and George turned around.

A tall blond woman dressed in a long black coat rushed up to Bess. She was holding a pad of paper and a pen. Nancy wasn't sure who she was. But she looked familiar.

"Bess Marvin, is it true that you lost the key to the city?" the woman demanded.

7

A Pink Clue

Bess stared at Nancy with a look of total panic.

How did this woman find out about the missing key? Nancy wondered.

Mrs. Marvin stepped up to the woman. "Excuse me, I'm Mrs. Marvin, Bess's mother. Who are you?"

The woman flashed a smile. "Alice Stone from *Today's Times*. Rumor has it that your daughter lost the key to the city. Any comment?"

"*Today's Times*. That's Brenda's dad's newspaper!" George whispered to Nancy.

"That big-mouthed Brenda must have blabbed my secret!" Bess whispered fiercely.

"How did it happen?" Ms. Stone prompted Bess as she scribbled in her pad. "Was it stolen? Do you know who did it?"

"We have no comment to make," Mrs. Marvin said huffily to the reporter.

The Marvins grabbed Bess by the hand and pulled her away from Alice Stone.

"Oh, my!" Hannah exclaimed to Nancy. "It's impossible to keep a secret from these reporters, isn't it?"

"Especially when Brenda Blabbermouth knows the secret too," George grumbled.

"Bess Marvin! Bess Marvin!"

Nancy turned around. A man was jogging down the sidewalk toward Bess. He had a microphone in his hand. Next to him was a young guy who was holding a TV camera. The camera had a logo on it: WRIV-TV.

"Oh, no, that's a TV reporter!" Bess moaned. "Everyone in River Heights is going to know that I lost the key to the city!"

The reporter stopped in front of Bess. "Casey Cameron, WRIV-TV," he said. "Which one of you is Bess Marvin? I'm wondering if I could get a comment from you about the missing key to the city!"

The Marvins looked angry. But before they could say a word, Nancy stepped up and smiled at Casey Cameron.

"I'm Nancy Drew, Bess's friend," she said. "Meet us at the Christmas tree when the tree-lighting ceremony starts. You'll get your story then!"

Before Casey Cameron could respond, Nancy grabbed Bess's arm and began walking in the other direction.

"Nancy, why did you tell the reporter that we'd have a story for him?" Bess whispered to Nancy as they hurried away.

"I just wanted to get rid of him for you," Nancy whispered back. "Besides, we *will* have a story for him. We'll find the key by then."

"How?" Bess moaned. "It's less than an hour till the tree-lighting ceremony. Mom and Dad said we have to tell Mr. Farnsworth really soon."

"We'll find it," Nancy said confidently.

But Nancy didn't feel as confident as she

sounded. Deep down, she wondered, *Is the key lost forever?*

Nancy knew that she had to put her worries aside, though. She made a quick plan. She told Bess and the others that she wanted to do one final sweep of the Ye Olde Antique Shoppe and the Book Nook.

They went to the Book Nook first. Ms. Sandback was there, handing out hot cider to customers. "I still haven't seen your shopping bag," she told them.

They all headed over to the antique store next. Mr. Ortiz's news wasn't any better. "Nope, no bag, and no key," he said.

Nancy thought that Mr. Ortiz wasn't acting guilty at all. Still, if he *was* the thief, he could be pretending to be innocent.

"Keep him busy," Nancy whispered to Bess and George. "Ask him to show you something up there." She pointed to some bookshelves near the counter.

Bess and George followed Nancy's instructions. While Mr. Ortiz's back was turned to her, Nancy quickly crossed the room. She wanted to check out the glass case with the antique keys again, and she didn't want

Mr. Ortiz to see her snooping around.

The display looked different from yesterday. There were some keys missing, and some new keys had been added.

But there was still no sign of Bess's key.

Nancy sighed in disappointment. It was beginning to look like Mr. Ortiz was not the thief. Maybe he just liked to keep a close watch over his antiques. Even worse, maybe the key *was* lost forever.

"It's time to head over to the tree!" Mr. Marvin announced, tapping his watch.

The group said good-bye to Mr. Ortiz and left the store. A few minutes later, they reached the tree. A huge crowd had gathered around it.

"Ten minutes till the tree-lighting ceremony," Mrs. Marvin said. "Bess, honey, I'm afraid you're going to have to tell Mr. Farnsworth the bad news and bow out of the ceremony."

"Oh, Mommy," Bess said, biting her lip.

Just then, Nancy spotted Melissa Adams and her family at the edge of the crowd.

Nancy noticed that Melissa's baby sister, Mandy, was pulling things out of her parents' shopping bags and tossing them down on the sidewalk.

Then Nancy noticed something else. Melissa was wearing fuzzy pink mittens. They looked like the ones Mr. Marvin bought for Bess at Muller's.

Nancy turned to Bess. "I know what happened to the key!" she said excitedly.

8

A Bright, Shiny Object

Bess squeezed Nancy's arm. "What do you mean you know what happened to the key?" she said breathlessly. "Did you find it?"

"What's going on?" George demanded.

Nancy dragged her friends over to where Melissa Adams was standing. "Melissa!" Nancy called out.

"Hey, guys," Melissa said, smiling.

"I know this is a strange question," Nancy said. "But where did you get those pink mittens!"

Bess stared at Melissa's mittens. "Oh, my gosh!" she exclaimed.

Melissa shrugged. "It's weird. My mom

bought me a pair of red mittens at Muller's on Friday. But when we got home, the bag had *pink* mittens in it. I don't know what happened. Maybe the salesclerk at Muller's mixed up my bag with someone else's."

"I think I know what happened," Nancy said with a grin.

"What?" Melissa asked her curiously.

"What?" Bess and George said in unison.

"On Friday, we ran into you at the Ye Olde Antique Shoppe—remember?" Nancy reminded Melissa. "Bess had a Muller's shopping bag with *pink* mittens in it. Melissa, you had a Muller's shopping bag with *red* mittens in it. I think the two bags got mixed up!"

"Oh, my gosh!" Melissa exclaimed again.

"I think this is what happened," Nancy went on. "On Friday, Bess put all her bags down for a second to check out some stuff at the store. Melissa put her Muller's bag down too. Then Melissa picked up Bess's Muller's bag by accident when she left the store. The other Muller's bag—the one with the red mittens—got left behind. And Mr. Ortiz found it. It's at his store right now!"

"Nancy, you're brilliant!" George cried out.

"Totally," Bess agreed. "Melissa, that means *you* have the key! It was in my Muller's bag, in a black velvet bag!"

"What key?" Melissa said, confused.

Nancy told Melissa all about the missing key. When she was finished, Melissa shook her head. "I don't have the key. When I got home that night, the only things I found in the shopping bag were the pink mittens!"

Nancy glanced over at Mandy, who was still digging through her parents' shopping bags. Something occurred to her.

"Melissa? Do you think maybe *Mandy* might have pulled the key out of the shopping bag?" Nancy said.

Melissa gasped. "Yes! On Friday night, after we left Mr. Ortiz's shop, I saw her chewing on something big and gold. I thought it was one of her toys. She has zillions of them. But maybe it was the key!"

"Where *exactly* did you see Mandy chewing on the gold thing?" Nancy asked her.

Melissa pointed to Star's Jewelers. "Right in front of Star's," she replied.

The four girls rushed over to the jewelry store, which was right next to the Christmas tree. "I think we know where the key is!" Nancy called out to her father.

Nancy and her friends searched all along the front of the jewelry store. After a few minutes, Nancy spotted something in a small mound of snow. It was the black velvet bag!

Nancy picked it up and shook the snow off it. She opened it and looked inside.

There was no key.

"It's not here," she said, disappointed.

The girls kept searching through the snow. The key was nowhere to be found. But the black bag meant that the key could be around somewhere. Nancy put the bag in her pocket.

A car horn honked. Nancy glanced up. A long, black limousine was pulling up in front of the Christmas tree.

The car door opened, and the mayor of River Heights stepped out. With him was Deputy Mayor Franklin Farnsworth.

"Oh, no, the ceremony is starting!" Bess cried out. "I'll *have* to tell the mayor now!"

Casey Cameron from WRIV-TV broke through the crowd. "We're coming to you live from the tree-lighting ceremony in River

Heights!" he said into his microphone. The cameraman hoisted his TV camera onto his shoulder. He turned on a bright light that lit up the tree while he got some footage of it.

Nancy glanced at the tree. The camera light shone off the many gold and silver ornaments that hung from the branches.

Then Nancy did a double take. Was she imagining things, or . . .

She ran to the tree and stood on her tiptoes. She plucked off one of the gold ornaments.

But it wasn't an ornament. It was the key to the city!

Bess rushed up to her. "Nancy, you found it!" she practically screamed. "Yay!"

George gave Nancy a high-five. "You are the most awesome detective in the world! How did you find it?"

"I saw it on the tree," Nancy said with a smile. She handed the key to Bess. "Quick! The ceremony is going to start! You have to give the key to the mayor!"

Bess nodded. "Okey-dokey!"

Melissa returned to her family. Nancy and George joined Mr. Drew and the others. "We found the key!" Nancy announced happily.

The ceremony started. The mayor read a speech about what a wonderful city River Heights was. At the end of the speech, he flicked on a switch. The entire Christmas tree lit up with tiny sparkling white lights!

Then the mayor handed the velvet bag to Bess. "Bess Marvin, you are charged with a very important job. The job of presenting the key to the city to Santa Claus!" he declared.

"Yes, sir, Mr. Mayor!" Bess said excitedly.

The sound of sleigh bells filled the air. Nancy turned around. Santa Claus and Mrs. Claus were driving up in a sleigh!

The crowd clapped and cheered. Nancy noticed that even Brenda, who was with her parents, was clapping.

The Clauses stopped and got out of their sleigh. "Santa Claus looks like he eats a lot of Christmas cookies," George remarked to Nancy. Nancy laughed.

The Clauses walked up to the tree, where Bess was standing. Bess did a little curtsy. "Santa Claus and Mrs. Claus, I hereby present you with a key to the city!" she said in a loud, clear voice.

Bess handed them the key. Santa Claus took it from her and kissed her cheek. Mrs. Claus did the same.

"Yay, Bess!" Nancy shouted.

"Way to go!" George cheered.

Nancy saw that Casey Cameron of WRIV-TV was getting it all on tape. And Alice Stone of *Today's Times* was scribbling like mad. But now, they only had happy news to report!

After the ceremony was over, the girls went to the Double Dip for hot chocolate. At the Double Dip, Nancy spotted Howard Nakamoto, who lived up the street, and a few other students from the junior high. They were sitting in a booth having hot-fudge sundaes.

Nancy tugged on Bess and George's hands. "Come on!" she said.

"What?" Bess said, looking confused.

"Let's go talk to Howard. He helped decorate the tree. Maybe he can tell us how the key got up there," Nancy explained.

"Where are you going?" Mr. Marvin asked.

"Be back in a sec, Daddy. Just order us

hot chocolate with lots and lots of whipped cream!" Bess said with a grin.

When Nancy, George, and Bess got to Howard's booth, they introduced themselves. "You live on my street," Nancy reminded him.

Howard nodded. "Oh, yeah. And you are the girl who gave the key to Santa tonight," he said pointing at Bess. Bess grinned. "These are my friends Lacey and Alex," Howard said, waving a hand at his friends. "They helped decorate the tree."

"We kind of wanted to ask you about that," Nancy said. "Do any of you remember putting a big gold key up on the tree?"

"That would be me," Howard replied.

"Where did you get it?" Bess asked him.

Howard shrugged. "It was kind of weird. I saw it on the ground in front of Star's Jewelers, just lying in the snow. I thought that maybe it fell out of the box of decorations or something. So I picked it up and put it on the tree."

"That key's been everywhere," Nancy said, grinning.

"What do you mean?" George asked her.

"Well, first, Bess had the key in her bag. Then Melissa picked up Bess's bag by accident. Then Melissa's sister, Mandy, took the key out of Melissa's bag. Then Mandy dropped it in front of Star's Jewelers. Then Howard found it and put it on the Christmas tree!" Nancy explained.

"That key sure went on a long trip!" Bess exclaimed.

Everyone laughed.

That night, Nancy opened up her blue detective notebook. She went to the page that said THE CASE OF THE MISSING KEY. She wrote:

I'm so glad we found the key in time. We didn't have a key thief at all. Our "thief" was a baby—Baby Mandy!

I guess if you have something superimportant to take care of, you should never let it out of your sight. Especially if it's the key to the city, and the mayor—and Santa Claus—are counting on you!

Case closed!